STAN LYNDE'S

PARDNERS

book two: the legacy

Other Books by Stan Lynde

A Month of Sundays - The Best of Rick O'Shay and Hipshot

Grass Roots

Pardners, Book One: The Bonding

Rick O'Shay, Hipshot, and Me

Available from:
Cottonwood Graphics
P.O. Box 848
Whitefish, MT 59937

STAN LYNDE'S

PARDNERS

book two: the legacy

COTTONWOOD
GRAPHICS, INC.

STAN LYNDE

Stan Lynde's PARDNERS ™
Book Two: The Legacy

Published by Cottonwood Graphics, Inc., Copyright © 1991
P.O. Box 848
Whitefish, Montana 59937

Printed in the United States of America

ISBN 0-9626999-2-6
LC # 90-84936

First Printing: December 1991

1 3 5 7 9 8 6 4 2

FOREWORD

Pardners, Book Two: The Legacy is the second book in a two-volume graphic novel designed to portray a somewhat different theme, and relationship between its principal characters, than may be usual in a "western" story.

I stated in the foreword to the first book, *Pardners, Book One: The Bonding* that my primary purpose was to entertain, and that beyond that immediate goal I hoped to express some positive points about courage, integrity, relationships, and the many aspects of love. How well those ambitions have been realized is for you, the reader, to judge, but I have been gratified and encouraged by the very favorable reactions to the first book. I hope that this, the continuation and conclusion of the story begun in that book, will be equally well-received, and I would very much appreciate any comments you may wish to share with me in that regard.

This book is a uniquely personal product, both in its writing and in its illustration. From start to finish, from concept to story to pencilling to lettering (with an assist from my intelligent but humorless computer/printer) to inking to the duo-tone shading and front and back covers, the work has been solely my own.

I very much hope you will enjoy this book, and that it will both interest and entertain you.

If it doesn't, at least you'll know who to blame.

Stan Lynde

WHAT HAS GONE BEFORE:

IN THE HIGH COUNTRY OF MONTANA TERRITORY, LONE WOLF FOOTLOOSE FAIRWEATHER IS JUST BEGINNING HIS EVENING MEAL WHEN SPUNKY, EIGHT-YEAR OLD FANCY FREE WANDERS INTO HIS CAMP, AND HIS LIFE. FANCY HAS LEFT THE DENVER HOME OF HER LESS THAN LOVING GUARDIANS, JINGLE AND JEZZIE BELL, TO LOOK FOR HER FATHER SCOTT FREE, WHO WENT NORTH THREE YEARS BEFORE TO SEEK HIS FORTUNE IN THE GOLD FIELDS.

FOOTLOOSE AND FANCY STRIKE A BARGAIN; HE WILL PROVIDE HER WITH ROOM, BOARD, AND EIGHT DOLLARS A MONTH IN RETURN FOR HER ASSUMING THE DUTIES OF COOK AND HOUSEKEEPER AT HIS REMOTE MOUNTAIN CABIN.

MEANWHILE, BACK IN DENVER, FANCY'S GUARDIANS ARE UNCONCERNED BY HER ABSENCE; "JINGLE", IN PARTICULAR, IS GLAD SHE'S GONE.

HIS ATTITUDE CHANGES, HOWEVER, WHEN A VISIT FROM AN ATTORNEY REVEALS THAT FANCY'S FATHER HAS BEEN KILLED IN AN ACCIDENT, THAT HE DIED A WEALTHY MAN, AND THAT HE LEFT HIS ENTIRE FORTUNE TO FANCY.

STALLING FOR TIME, THE BELLS TELL THE LAWYER THAT FANCY IS AWAY "VISITING FRIENDS" BUT THAT THEY WILL BRING HER TO HIS OFFICE SOON.

FACED NOW BY THE URGENT NEED TO FIND THEIR RUNAWAY WARD, THE BELLS HIRE PRIVATE DETECTIVE SNAVELY PEEPERS TO LOCATE HER AND BRING HER BACK TO DENVER.

IN MONTANA, FOOTLOOSE AND FANCY HAVE FOUND THAT THEIR INITIAL WORKING ARRANGEMENT HAS BECOME A RELATIONSHIP OF GENUINE FRIENDSHIP AND LOVE; THEY HAVE BECOME "PARDNERS" AND FAMILY.

ON A TRIP TO THE TOUGH TOWN OF HOOLIGAN, FOOTLOOSE LEARNS OF SCOTT FREE'S DEATH, AND WITH A HEAVY HEART BREAKS THE NEWS TO FANCY. HE COMFORTS HER AS SHE GRIEVES AND TELLS HER SOMETHING OF HIS OWN PAST, INCLUDING TIME SPENT IN PRISON AS A YOUNG MAN.

"THAT'S WHERE AH LEARNED ABOUT THE WAY HOPE HURTS WHEN IT DIES," HE TELLS HER, "AND ABOUT BEIN' ALONE."

"I GUESS WE BOTH LEARNED TO BE LONERS," SHE REPLIES, "BUT I THINK BEIN' FAMILY IS GONNA BE A LOT MORE FUN."

Hooligan, Montana Territory..
TELEGRAM FOR YOU, SANDY..FROM DENVER!
THANKS, BURT..

SHERIFF SANDY STONE
HOOLIGAN, MONTANA TERRITORY

SEEKING INFORMATION AS TO WHEREABOUTS
MINOR FEMALE CHILD, AGE ABOUT EIGHT
YEARS, HAIR BLONDE, EYES BLUE, NAME
FANCY FREE. IF KNOWN YOUR AREA
PLEASE CONTACT

SNAVELY PEEPERS
PRIVATE INVESTIGATOR
DENVER

HOLD THE FORT, WAYLON.. I'VE GOT TO TAKE ME A RIDE OUT TO FOOTLOOSE FAIRWEATHER'S PLACE..I'LL BE BACK IN THE MORNIN'.

YOU AIN'T BEEN AS HONEST WITH ME AS YOU MIGHT'VE BEEN, FOOTLOOSE..
THAT GIRL'S NAME AIN'T FAIRWEATHER, IT'S FREE..

..AND SHE AIN'T YOUR BROTHER'S CHILD, BECAUSE ACCORDIN' TO YOUR PRISON RECORDS YOU DON'T HAVE A BROTHER.

NOW I DON'T MIND BEIN' LIED TO NOW AN' AGAIN, BUT IT DOES MAKE ME WONDER WHY YOU FIGURED IT WAS NECESSARY.

YOU'RE JUST IN TIME FOR SUPPER, SHERIFF.. GET DOWN AND REST YOUR BIG, FAT..HORSE.

WHAT BRINGS YOU OUT THIS WAY, SANDY..KIND OF FAR FROM THE BRIGHT LIGHTS OF THE CITY FOR YOU, AIN'T IT?
I'M HERE ON BUSINESS, FOOTLOOSE.. I NEED A FEW QUESTIONS ANSWERED.

WULL..SET DOWN AND ASK AWAY, SANDY. CAN I OFFER YOU A DRINK, OR ARE YOU ON DUTY?
THE ANSWER IS YES..TO BOTH QUESTIONS.

I GOT A TELEGRAM THIS MORNIN'..FROM DENVER. SEEMS SOME PRIVATE DETECTIVE IS LOOKIN' FOR A MISSIN' YOUNGSTER..BY THE NAME OF FANCY.

SHE'S DESCRIBED AS BEIN' ABOUT EIGHT YEARS OLD, HAVIN' BLUE EYES AND BLONDE HAIR. SOUNDS A LOT LIKE YOUR NIECE, DON'T SHE?
ALL RIGHT, SANDY.. FANCY'S NOT MAH NIECE..

..SHE WANDERED INTO MAH CAMP A FEW WEEKS BACK, RUNNIN' FROM BAD TROUBLE AT HOME..
2.

..SHE'S HERE BECAUSE SHE WANTS TO BE. WE'RE PARDNERS, SANDY.. FAMILY.
THAT'S RIGHT, SHERIFF.. I'M NEVER GOIN' BACK TO WHERE I CAME FROM.

THAT'S PRETTY CLEAR. I RECKON YOU HAVE YOUR REASONS..

..BUT I AM GONNA HAVE TO LET THIS PEEPERS FELLER KNOW SHE'S HERE. AS FAR AS I'M CONCERNED, THAT'S THE END OF IT..UNLESS I SEE SOME LEGAL PAPER.
THAT'S FAIR ENOUGH, SANDY..

..BUT AH RECKON YOU NEED TO KNOW WHERE WE STAND. AH'LL CONSIDER ANYBODY WHO COMES HERE HUNTIN' FANCY A TRESPASSER.. UNLESS YOU'RE WITH 'EM..

..AND AH CAN JUST ABOUT GUARANTEE THEY WON'T BE GLAD THEY CAME.

3

SHERIFF STONE? I'M SNAVELY PEEPERS.. I RECEIVED YOUR TELEGRAM REGARDING THE MINOR CHILD FANCY FREE..

..AND I CAUGHT THE FIRST COACH OUT OF DENVER. I'M HERE TO TAKE HER BACK, AND I'D APPRECIATE YOUR COOPERATION, SHERIFF.
WELL, SHE IS IN THE AREA, PEEPERS.. LIVIN' WITH A MAN NAME O' FOOTLOOSE FAIRWEATHER..

..BUT SHE SEEMS INCLINED TO STAY WHERE SHE IS. DO YOU HAVE A COURT ORDER FOR THE CHILD?
WHY..NO. MY CLIENTS DIDN'T THINK THAT WOULD BE NECESSARY.

YOUR CLIENTS WERE WRONG, PEEPERS..IT'S DANG SURE NECESSARY IF YOU WANT MY HELP.
YOU'RE A SWORN PEACE OFFICER, SHERIFF..IT'S YOUR JOB TO SEE JUSTICE DONE.

I DON'T NEED NO SLICK-TALKIN' DENVER SNOOP TO TELL ME WHAT MY JOB IS, PEEPERS..I'M THE ONLY LAW WITHIN 60 MILES, AND I TEND TO DECIDE WHAT NEEDS DOIN' HEREABOUTS!
I'M TELLIN' YOU ONCE MORE.. IF YOU DON'T HAVE A COURT ORDER YOU'VE MADE A LONG TRIP FOR NOTHIN'.
I SEE. THEN I SUPPOSE I SHALL HAVE TO GO ALONE. WHERE CAN I FIND THIS FOOTLOOSE FAIRWEATHER?

4.

HE'S GOT A CABIN ABOUT TEN MILES NORTH O' HERE, WHERE TEPEE CREEK JOINS WALKIN' WOLF RIVER. YOU CAN RENT A SADDLEHORSE AT THE LIVERY STABLE UP THE STREET..

..BUT I'D THINK TWICE ABOUT GOIN' UP THERE IF I WAS YOU. IF HE DECIDES YOU'RE A TRESPASSER, I'LL HAVE TO FETCH YOU BACK ACROSS A PACKHORSE AND BURY YOU AT COUNTY EXPENSE. THAT'D BE A REAL INCONVENIENCE TO ME.

SOMEBODY'S COMIN', FOOTLOOSE.

THAT'S FAR ENOUGH, STRANGER..REIN UP AND STATE YOUR BUSINESS.
EASY, MISTER.. I MEAN YOU NO HARM..

..I'M SNAVELY PEEPERS, FROM DENVER. SHERIFF STONE TOLD ME YOU HAVE A MINOR FEMALE CHILD LIVING HERE WITH YOU.
SOMETIMES A MAN FINDS MORE THAN HE'S LOOKIN' FOR, PEEPERS..
I'M LOOKING FOR SUCH A CHILD..NAME OF FANCY FREE.

5.

..SO AH'D ADVISE YOU TO GO ON BACK T' DENVER BEFORE THAT HAPPENS T' YOU.
THERE IN THE DOORWAY BEHIND YOU..IS YOUR NAME FANCY FREE, CHILD?
YOU'VE PURELY WORE OUT YOUR WELCOME, PEEPERS..AH WANT YOU OFF MAH PLACE, WHILE YOU CAN STILL RIDE..
..HE TAKES HIS HAT OFF!
BLAM!
..AND WHILE AH'M STILL IN A GOOD MOOD.

AH DON'T KNOW HOW IT IS WHERE YOU COME FROM, MISTER..BUT OUT HERE, WHEN A MAN SPEAKS TO A LADY..

WELL, MR. PEEPERS? YOU SAID YOU HAD SOMETHING TO TELL ME?
INDEED I DO, MR. BELL.. I BELIEVE I HAVE FOUND YOUR MISSING WARD.
BAVELY PEEPERS PRIVATE

YOU'VE FOUND FANCY? GOOD WORK! WHERE IS SHE?
PATIENCE, MR. BELL.. LET ME COMPLETE MY REPORT.

FIRST, I CHECKED WITH ALL THE LOCAL RAIL AND STAGECOACH LINES, BUT WITHOUT SUCCESS..

..AND THEN I MADE CONTACT WITH PEACE OFFICERS IN MONTANA AND WYOMING TERRITORIES.
DENVER

ONE, A CERTAIN SHERIFF SANDY STONE, REPLIED IN THE AFFIRMATIVE. THERE IS INDEED A CHILD ANSWERING FANCY'S DESCRIPTION, NEWLY ARRIVED IN MONTANA TERRITORY..

..SHE RESIDES NEAR THE TOWN OF HOOLIGAN WITH A RATHER DANGEROUS MAN CALLED FOOTLOOSE FAIRWEATHER. I VISITED HIS CABIN AND SAW THE CHILD.

HOWEVER, WHEN I ASKED HER IF SHE WAS INDEED FANCY FREE, FAIRWEATHER SHOT THE HAT OFF MY HEAD AND THREATENED MY LIFE. I'M NOT A PHYSICALLY COURAGEOUS..OR FOOLHARDY MAN, MR. BELL..
THEREFORE, I HEREBY RESIGN FROM THE CASE AND PRESENT THIS BILL FOR SERVICES RENDERED. GOOD LUCK, SIR..YOU'RE GOING TO NEED IT.

I'M BODIE SLAGG, MISTER.. BARKEEP SAID YOU WANTED TO SEE ME.
THAT'S RIGHT. CAN I BUY YOU A DRINK?

DON'T MIND IF I DO, FRIEND..I'VE DONE FELL ON HARD TIMES LATELY.
I'M HERE TO CHANGE ALL THAT, SLAGG..I JUST MAY HAVE A JOB FOR YOU.

WELL, I AIN'T ALL THAT PARTICULAR, MISTER..BUT WHAT KIND O' JOB WOULD THAT BE?
DOES IT MATTER? I'M TOLD YOU'LL DO ALMOST ANYTHING FOR MONEY.

AIN'T NO "ALMOST" TO IT, FRIEND.. YOU PAY FOR IT AND I'LL DO IT. WHAT'S THE JOB?

I NEED YOU TO GO UP TO MONTANA TERRITORY AND BRING BACK A LITTLE GIRL. PROBLEM IS, SHE DOESN'T WANT TO COME BACK.

8.

SECOND PROBLEM IS SHE'S LIVIN' WITH A TOUGH GENT WHO DOESN'T WANT HER TO COME BACK EITHER.
UH-HUH. WHAT DO YOU FIGGER THEM TWO PROBLEMS ARE WORTH?
LET'S SAY..FIVE HUNDRED DOLLARS A PROBLEM, IN GOLD COIN.
FIVE HUNDRED EACH, HUH?
GIMME TWO HUNDRED IN ADVANCE, AND A BOTTLE O' THIS GOOD WHISKEY, AND I'LL LEAVE THIS MORNIN'.
KENTUCKY
THAT'S RIGHT, JEZZIE..I'VE LOCATED OUR DARLING FANCY, AND I'VE MADE ARRANGEMENTS TO HAVE HER BROUGHT BACK HERE.
YOU'VE FOUND HER? IS..IS SHE ALL RIGHT?
I DIDN'T THINK TO ASK, JEZ. THE POINT IS, SHE'S BEEN FOUND AND WE'LL SOON HAVE HER BACK IN OUR HANDS..
..WHICH MEANS WE'LL SOON HAVE HER INHERITANCE IN OUR HANDS.
BUT WHAT IF SHE WON'T COOPERATE, JINGLE?
OH, SHE'LL COOPERATE, JEZ..AND WHEN I GET THROUGH WITH THAT YOUNG LADY, SHE WON'T BE RUNNING AWAY AGAIN, EITHER.
SALE
BEER
SALOON
CIGARS
IRCUS AUG. 3-5
EXTRAVAGANZA
9.

SUPPER'S ALMOST READY, FOOTLOOSE..YOU HUNGRY?
SURE AM, PUNKIN'..

..BUT AH'M GONNA HAVE TO SADDLE OLD BRUTUS AND CHECK ON THE HORSES IN THE SOUTH PASTURE FIRST.

AH STAKED 'EM OUT THIS MORNIN', BUT THEY'VE BEEN ACTIN' A MITE NERVOUS. COULD BE THERE'S A BEAR AROUND.

BE BACK IN A BIT, KEEP THEM BISCUITS WARM, LITTLE DARLIN'.

WELL, NOW..LOOKS LIKE MY LUCK'S CHANGIN' AT LAST! THE BIG FELLER'S RIDIN' OUT, AND THE YOUNG'UN IS STAYIN' BEHIND!
10.

I WONDER WHAT'S KEEPIN' FOOTLOOSE..SUPPER'S GONNA GET COLD.
GOTCHA, KID!
POW!
POW!
HUH?
AH'M COMIN', FANCY!

KAPOW!
FOOTLOOSE!
FOOTLOOSE! YOU SHOT FOOTLOOSE!
HAD TO, SIS.. NOW YOU HUSH!

12.

HERE'S HOW IT'S GONNA BE, SIS..YOU'RE GONNA GET YOUR STUFF TOGETHER AN' THEN I'M TAKIN' YOU BACK T' DENVER..
..NOW WE CAN DO IT EASY, WITH YOU BEIN' QUIET AND WILLIN'..OR WE CAN DO IT THE HARD WAY..
..WHICH MEANS I'LL HAVE T' HURT YOU SOME. BUT BELIEVE ME, SIS..EITHER WAY, WE'RE GOIN'.
13.

UNH..'RECKON AH'M STILL ALIVE.. FAR AS AH KNOW, DEAD FOLK DON'T FEEL PAIN..

HEAD..FEELS LIKE SOME BIG BLACKSMITH IS USIN' IT FOR A ANVIL..

DIZZY, TOO.. LIGHT-HEADED. GOT TO GET TO MAH HORSE..

EASY.. STEADY, BRUTUS.. DON'T SPOOK ON ME NOW.

FANCY'S GONE..THAT BIG GENT WITH THE RIFLE MUST'VE TOOK HER.. TO DENVER, MORE'N LIKELY..

WULL..IF EVER'BODY ELSE IS GOIN' TRAVELIN', AH RECKON AH WILL TOO.

J.D. CUTTER M.D.
FOOTLOOSE! WHAT IN THE WORLD HAPPENED TO YOU?
HAD..ME A LITTLE ACCIDENT, DOC..

A LITTLE ACCIDENT, EH? WELL, I HOPE YOU NEVER HAVE A BIG ONE.. YOU'VE LOST A LOT OF BLOOD.
AH'VE GOT ENOUGH LEFT TO DO WHAT AH HAVE T' DO, DOC.

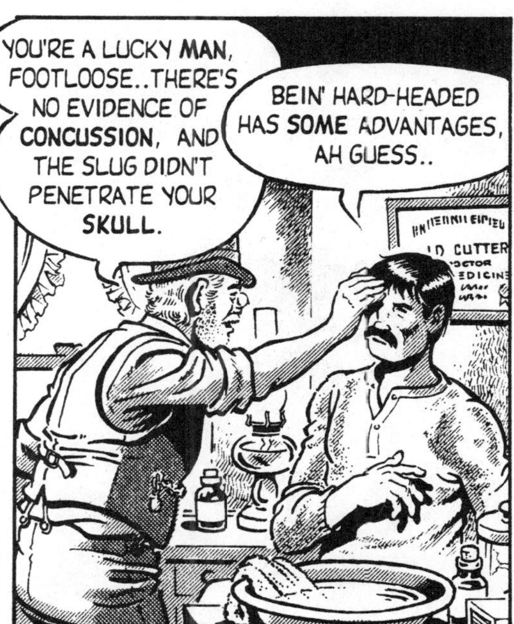

YOU'RE A LUCKY MAN, FOOTLOOSE..THERE'S NO EVIDENCE OF CONCUSSION, AND THE SLUG DIDN'T PENETRATE YOUR SKULL.
BEIN' HARD-HEADED HAS SOME ADVANTAGES, AH GUESS..
J.D. CUTTER DOCTOR MEDICINE

YOU'LL HAVE TO TAKE IT EASY FOR AWHILE..NO HEAVY WORK, AND PLENTY OF BED REST.
APPRECIATE THE DOCTORIN' BUT AH CAN'T USE THE ADVICE, SAWBONES..
J.D CUTT DOCTOR MEDICIN

..BUT DON'T WORRY.. AH FIGURE TO PAY YOU FOR BOTH.

15.

SHE'S HERE, JEZZIE.. SLAGG BROUGHT HER BACK!

WELCOME HOME, CHILD.. CAN'T SAY WE'VE MISSED YOU.

GOOD WORK, SLAGG.. DID SHE GIVE YOU ANY TROUBLE?
SHE DIDN'T, BUT HER COWBOY FRIEND TRIED TO..

I LEFT HIM HEAD-SHOT IN FRONT OF HIS CABIN, AND FETCHED THE YOUNGUN' HERE.
YOU'VE EARNED YOUR PAY, SLAGG.

LOCK HER IN HER ROOM, JEZ.. I'LL BE UP IN A MINUTE. MR. SLAGG AND I HAVE SOME BUSINESS TO DISCUSS.
16.

HERE'S THE THOUSAND I OWE YOU.. YOU DID A GOOD JOB.

THERE'S ANOTHER TWO HUNDRED IN IT FOR YOU IF YOU'LL STICK AROUND THIS WEEK AND HELP KEEP AN EYE ON THE BRAT.
I AIN'T NO WET NURSE, JINGLE..

..BUT ME AND THE KID DO HAVE AN UNDERSTANDIN' AND I CAN USE THE MONEY. IT'S A DEAL.

WELL, YOUNG LADY..YOU'VE CAUSED US A GREAT DEAL OF TROUBLE AND EXPENSE, BUT NOW IT'S PAYBACK TIME.
WHY DID YOU BRING ME BACK? YOU DON'T CARE ABOUT ME..

..I FOUND SOMEONE WHO DID, AND I WAS HAPPY..BUT THAT AWFUL MR. SLAGG SHOT HIM!
YOU'RE RIGHT, FANCY..I DON'T CARE ABOUT YOU..
..BUT IT TURNS OUT YOU'RE WORTH A GREAT DEAL OF MONEY, AND YOU'RE GOING TO HELP US GET IT.
17.

WHAT DID JINGLE MEAN ABOUT MY BEING WORTH A LOT OF MONEY, AUNT JEZZIE? DO YOU HATE ME, TOO?
WHY, NO, CHILD.. I DON'T HATE YOU..

..JUST EAT YOUR SUPPER NOW AND GO TO BED. IF YOU BEHAVE, HE WON'T HURT YOU.

..BUT YOU KNOW HOW JINGLE IS..HE CAN BE SO CRUEL SOMETIMES. I..I CAN'T GO AGAINST HIM..

DEAR MISTER GOD.. I REALLY NEED YOUR HELP, SIR..I DON'T KNOW WHAT TO DO..

..THAT BAD MISTER SLAGG SHOT FOOTLOOSE AND BROUGHT ME TO THESE AWFUL PEOPLE..AND I.. I'M SCARED, LORD..

..PLEASE HELP ME AND KEEP ME SAFE. I SURE WOULD APPRECIATE IT. AMEN.

18.

FIVE-THIRTY..TIME TO CLOSE UP AND GO HOME.
SNAVELY PEEPERS PRIVATE INVESTIGATOR
THINGS HAVE BEEN SLOW LATELY, ANYWAY..
EVENIN', PEEPERS!
FAIRWEATHER!
NOW AH AIN'T KNOWN FOR MAH PATIENCE, SO AH'M ONLY GONNA ASK YOU ONCE.. WHERE CAN I FIND JINGLE BELL?
I..I'LL TELL! DON'T HURT ME!
332 COLUMBUS STREET..WEST SIDE OF TOWN!
UH-HUH. THAT BETTER BE THE RIGHT ADDRESS, PILGRIM..
..BUT JUST IN CASE IT'S NOT, OR YOU PLAN ON SEEIN' JINGLE BEFORE AH DO, AH'M GONNA TIE YOU UP SOME.

IS THE BRAT IN BED, JEZZIE?
YES.. SHE IS..

..BUT SHE'S SO FRIGHTENED AND HELPLESS. DO WE HAVE TO BE SO COLD AND CRUEL TOWARD HER?
WE NEED THAT MONEY, JEZ..AND WE NEED HER SCARED ENOUGH TO HELP US GET IT.

THAT MONEY'S NOT JUST FOR ME, YOU KNOW..YOUR BOOZE HABIT IS GETTING MORE EXPENSIVE ALL THE TIME..

..AND I DON'T KNOW HOW YOU COULD AFFORD IT IF I WASN'T AROUND TO PAY THE BILLS.
NOW I DON'T WANT ANY MORE HEARTS AN' FLOWERS ABOUT THAT KID, JEZ.. DO YOU HEAR ME?
Y-YES JINGLE.

KNOCK, KNOCK! CAN AH COME IN?
FAIRWEATHER!
20.

WE AIN'T MET, BUT AH RECKON YOU'D BE JINGLE BELL..

..YOU'VE GOT THAT SNEAKIN', GUTLESS MEAN LOOK AH FIGURED YOU'D HAVE.
FAIRWEATHER! BUT YOU..YOU'RE..

DEAD? NOT HARDLY, JINGLE..EVEN THOUGH THAT SKULKIN' PIECE O' TRAIL TRASH YOU SENT TRIED T' DO ME IN. THAT'S WHAT COMES OF HIRIN' CHEAP HELP.

AH'M HERE FOR FANCY..AH'M TAKIN' HER BACK HOME, AND YOU'VE GOT ABOUT TWO MINUTES TO BRING HER OUT.
THAT'S NOT MUCH TIME, FAIRWEATHER..BUT YOU HAVE EVEN LESS THAN THAT..

BEFORE MY MAN BODIE CUTS YOU IN HALF WITH HIS SCATTERGUN!
KLIK!

21.

I BELIEVE YOU GENTLEMEN HAVE ALREADY MET..TAKE HIS GUN, BODIE!
YOU SHOULD'VE STAYED ON YOUR BELLY IN THAT MEADOW, COWBOY!
SHUT YOUR MOUTH!
WHOK!
FOOTLOOSE!

IF YOU'D BEEN A BETTER SHOT, AH MIGHT HAVE.. BUT THEN YOU MOSTLY FIGHT LITTLE GIRLS, DON'CHA, BODIE?
DRAG THAT YOKEL INTO THE OTHER ROOM, BODIE, AND TIE HIM UP..
..AND YOU, MISSY, SIT DOWN AND SHUT UP!
I'M ONLY GOING TO SAY THIS ONCE, LITTLE LADY, SO LISTEN CLOSE! YOU'RE HERE BECAUSE WE NEED YOUR HELP..

22.

..AND YOU'RE GOING TO DO EXACTLY AS WE SAY, OR YOUR COWBOY FRIEND IS A DEAD MAN.. UNDERSTAND?
Y..YES.

ALL RIGHT. NOW YOUR FATHER, SCOTT FREE, DIED LAST WINTER..AND HE DIED RICH. HE LEFT EVERYTHING TO YOU, HIS ONLY CHILD..

..BUT BECAUSE YOU'RE A MINOR, SOMEONE ELSE WILL BE NAMED TO HANDLE YOUR ESTATE. JEZZIE AND I INTEND TO BE THAT SOMEONE!

DON'T KID YOURSELF, GIRL.. WE DON'T LIKE YOU ANY BETTER THAN YOU LIKE US, BUT WE'RE STILL YOUR LEGAL GUARDIANS..

..AND MAKE NO MISTAKE ABOUT IT, YOU ARE GOING TO HELP US GET THAT MONEY!

23.

NOW YOU'RE BEIN' SENSIBLE.
I..I'LL DO WHATEVER YOU WANT ME TO. JUST DON'T HURT FOOTLOOSE..

IT'S ONLY MONEY WE'RE TALKIN' ABOUT, AFTER ALL..AND WHAT WOULD A KID LIKE YOU DO WITH ALL THAT WEALTH?

KEEP AN EYE ON HER, JEZZIE..I'M GOING TO SEE THAT LAWYER AND SET UP A COURT HEARING.
YES, JINGLE..

AUNT JEZZIE..DO YOU REALLY FEEL THE WAY JINGLE DOES? YOU WERE MAMA'S FRIEND! I CAN'T BELIEVE YOU..
I..I CAN'T GO AGAINST HIM, FANCY..

..WE DO NEED THAT MONEY. I..I HAVEN'T BEEN WELL.. AND WE HAVE SO MANY DEBTS..
YEAH..
Jingle

WELL..I SUPPOSE IT COULDN'T HURT..
COULD I TALK TO FOOTLOOSE? I JUST WANT TO BE SURE HE'S ALL RIGHT.

HULLO, PUNKIN'..HOW ARE YOU DOIN?
I'M ALL RIGHT.. HOW ARE YOU?

WULL..AH HAVE BEEN BETTER, BUT THEN IT SEEMS LIKE WHENEVER AH GO TO THE BIG CITY AH GET TORE UP A MITE.

THE WORST PART IS HAVIN' T' SET HERE LOOKIN' AT OL' BODIE YONDER.. HE SURE AIN'T THE PURTIEST SIGHT AH EVER SAW..

BUT DON'T YOU GO WORRYIN' ABOUT ME. AH'VE BEEN IN TIGHT PLACES BEFORE. JUST YOU TAKE CARE OF YOURSELF, LITTLE DARLIN'.
ALL RIGHT..THAT'S ENOUGH! GET AWAY FROM HIM, GIRL!

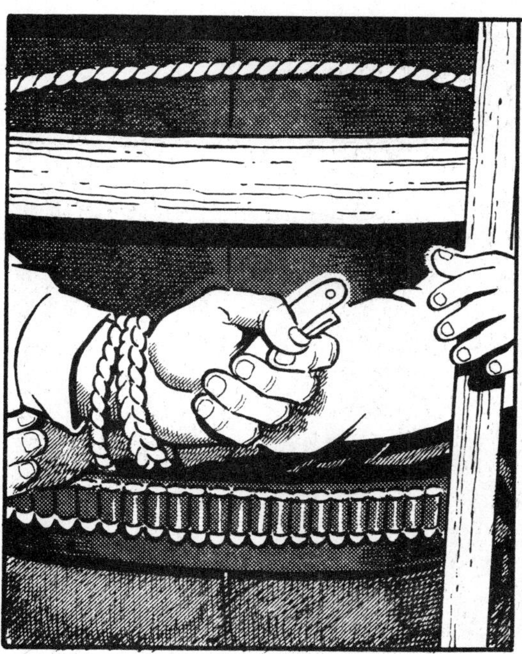

EVERYTHING'S GONNA BE ALL RIGHT, FOOTLOOSE.
WHY, YES, FANCY.. AH BELIEVE YOU'RE RIGHT.

25.

EVERYTHING'S SET, JEZ.. WE MEET THE LAWYER AT TEN, AND GO TO COURT AT ONE THIS AFTERNOON. BRING THE KID AND LET'S GO!
YES, JINGLE.

KEEP A TIGHT EYE ON THE COWBOY, BODIE.. ARE YOU SURE THOSE ROPES ARE TIGHT ENOUGH?
WHEN I TIE EM' THEY STAY TIED, JINGLE.

..AN DON'T WORRY..IF HE EVEN LOOKS WRONG I'LL CUT HIM IN HALF WITH THIS SCATTERGUN.
GOOD MAN, BODIE.. THERE JUST MAY BE A BONUS IN ALL THIS FOR YOU!

REMEMBER, FANCY.. WHAT HAPPENS TO FOOTLOOSE DEPENDS ON YOU.
I UNDERSTAND.
DENVER C
PRINTING OFFI

AH! MR. AND MRS. BELL! YOU'RE RIGHT ON TIME! AND THIS MUST BE OUR LITTLE HEIRESS!
YES..THIS IS FANCY FREE, OUR WARD. FANCY, THIS IS LAWYER NOLO CONTENDERE.

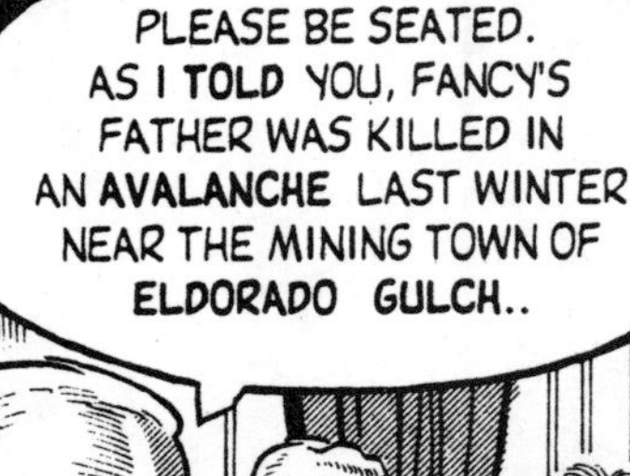

PLEASE BE SEATED. AS I TOLD YOU, FANCY'S FATHER WAS KILLED IN AN AVALANCHE LAST WINTER NEAR THE MINING TOWN OF ELDORADO GULCH..

..AND HE LEFT HIS ENTIRE WORLDLY GOODS TO YOU, MISS FREE. YOUR GUARDIANS HAVE PETITIONED THE COURT TO BE APPOINTED EXECUTORS OF YOUR ESTATE..

..AND WE WILL APPEAR IN COURT THIS AFTERNOON, WHERE JUDGE PRUDENCE WILL RENDER HIS DECISION. ANY QUESTIONS?
UH.. CAN YOU TELL US HOW MUCH THE INHERITANCE IS?

ONLY APPROXIMATELY, I'M AFRAID. HIS WILL, A KEY, AND A SMALL LOCKED CHEST WERE DELIVERED TO ME LAST MONTH..

..WITH THE PROVISION THAT ONLY HIS BENEFICIARY FANCY UNLOCK IT IN THE PRESENCE OF THE JUDGE.

BUT HIS PARTNER, WHO DELIVERED THE CHEST, ASSURES ME HIS BEQUEST IS APPROXIMATELY $50,000. DOES THAT ANSWER YOUR QUESTION, MR. BELL?
OH, YES..INDEED IT DOES! THANK YOU!

THEN, IF THERE ARE NO FURTHER QUESTIONS, I'LL SEE YOU AT THE COURTHOUSE AT ONE.
THANKS AGAIN.. WE'LL BE THERE!
27.

I GUESS YOU AIN'T GOIN' ANYWHERE..I'M GONNA SEE IF OLD JINGLE'S GOT ANOTHER BOTTLE HID OUT SOMEWHERES.
AW, YOU DON'T HAVE T' DO THAT JUST FOR ME, BODIE.

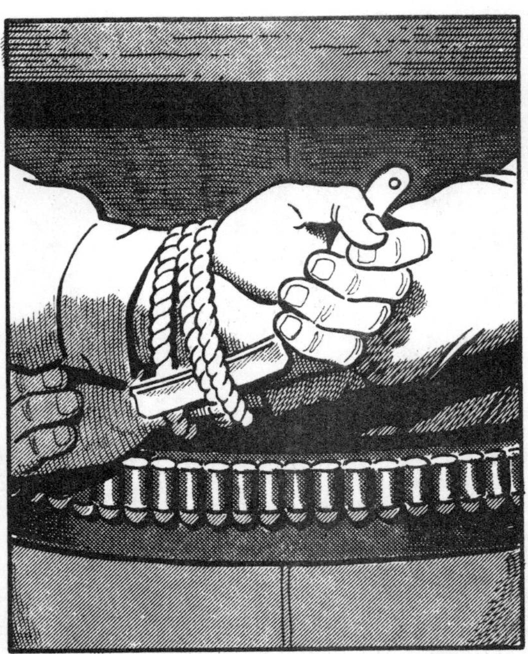

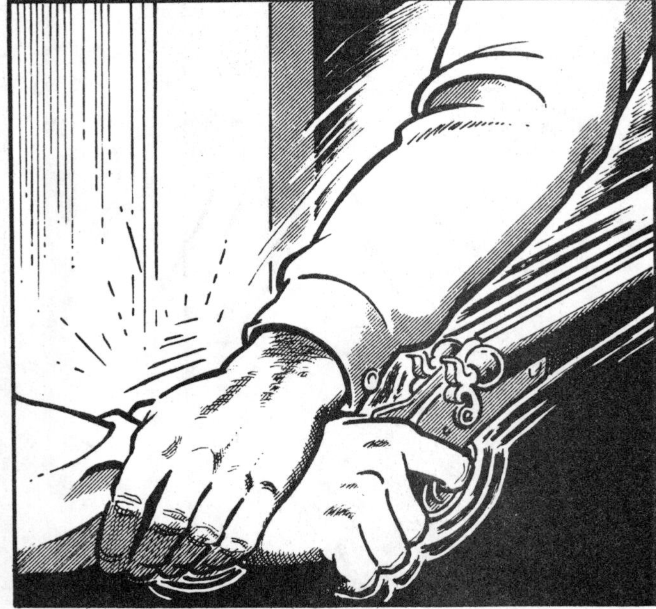

28.

WHUMP!
KRAK!
THAT'S RIGHT.. YOU JUST SET AN' REST AWHILE..

AH'M SORRY..TIME'S UP. AH'M SORT OF IN A HURRY, BODIE..GET YOUR CLOTHES OFF..DOWN TO YOUR LONG-JOHNS.
WHAT THE..?
ONCE YOU'RE DISROBED AH'M GONNA START YOU RUNNIN' THROUGH THE STREETS OF DENVER..

..AND IF YOU RUN REAL FAST YOU MIGHT EVEN BE ABLE T' OUTRUN THE BUCKSHOT.
FLINK!

29

YOU..YOU CAN'T MAKE ME GO OUT THERE IN THE STREET WITHOUT NO CLOTHES..
NO, AH GUESS THAT'S UP T' YOU, BODIE..

..BUT IF IT WAS ME, AH DRUTHER BE A LITTLE COLD AND EMBARRASSED THAN DEAD. NOW, MOVE!

BLAM!

ROOMS

LOOKS LIKE OL' BODIE IS IN GOOD HANDS..BUT HE IS GONNA HAVE SOME EXPLAININ' T' DO..
DRY GOODS

..AND AH NEED T' GO DOWNTOWN MAHSELF, BUT AH BELIEVE AH'LL DO IT WITH MAH CLOTHES ON!
30

YOUR HONOR..MY CLIENTS, MR. AND MRS. BELL, HAVE COME HERE TODAY WITH THEIR WARD, MISS FANCY FREE..

..TO PETITION THE COURT THAT THEY BE NAMED EXECUTORS OF MISS FREE'S ESTATE. THEY ARE PRESENTLY HER LEGAL GUARDIANS.
I SEE. THIS WOULD SEEM TO BE A RELATIVELY SIMPLE CASE, COUNSELOR..

..THE PETITION IS UNCONTESTED, AND..AS YOU POINTED OUT, THE BELLS ARE THE LEGAL GUARDIANS OF THE GIRL.

DOES ANYONE HERE HAVE ANYTHING THEY'D LIKE TO SAY BEFORE I RENDER MY DECISION? MISS FREE?

'SCUSE ME FOR BEIN' LATE, JUDGE.. BUT AH WAS TIED UP!
FOOTLOOSE!

YES, JUDGE..YOU BET YOUR SWEET LIFE I HAVE SOMETHING TO SAY!

ORDER! ORDER! RESTRAIN THAT MAN, BAILIFF! WHO IS HE, ANYWAY?
I'LL TELL YOU WHO HE IS, JUDGE..HE'S FOOTLOOSE FAIRWEATHER, MY FRIEND!

..AND THESE SO-CALLED GUARDIANS ARE A COUPLE OF CHEAP CROOKS!
TELL 'EM FANCY!

DON'T LISTEN TO HER, JUDGE..SHE'S LYING! SHE..
SILENCE!

BAILIFF..MAKE CERTAIN NO ONE LEAVES THE COURTROOM! MISS FREE.. COME WITH ME..I'LL SPEAK TO YOU IN CHAMBERS!
YES, YOUR HONOR!

YOU LOOK SORTER NERVOUS, JINGLE..WANT ME T' SEND OUT FOR SOME SMELLIN' SALTS?

ALL RISE! THE HONORABLE JURRIS PRUDENCE PRESIDING!
GO AHEAD AND TAKE YOUR SEAT, FANCY.

MR. AND MRS. BELL.. IT IS DIFFICULT FOR ME TO EXPRESS MY FEELINGS AT THIS MOMENT..

..EXCEPT TO SAY THAT IF EVEN HALF OF WHAT MISS FREE HAS TOLD ME IS TRUE, YOU SHOULD BOTH BE CONFINED TO PRISON ON CRIMINAL CHARGES..

..INCLUDING PHYSICAL AND MENTAL ABUSE OF A MINOR CHILD, EXTORTION, FRAUD, KIDNAPPING, AND ASSAULT..

..NOT TO MENTION YOUR MOST SERIOUS FAILING..ALTHOUGH IT IS NOT IN ITSELF A CRIME.. TERMINAL GREED!

I'M GOING TO POSTPONE THIS HEARING UNTIL ONE O'CLOCK TOMORROW, AT WHICH TIME I'LL RENDER MY DECISION.

MEANWHILE, I INTEND TO CONDUCT A THOROUGH INVESTIGATION OF MISS FREE'S MOST SERIOUS ALLEGATIONS AGAINST MR. AND MRS. BELL. COURT IS ADJOURNED!

FANCY..MR. FAIRWEATHER.. WILL YOU PLEASE REMAIN? I'D LIKE TO SPEAK FURTHER WITH YOU BOTH.

I'D LIKE TO KNOW A BIT MORE ABOUT YOU, MR. FAIRWEATHER.. WHAT DO YOU DO FOR A LIVING?
MOSTLY, AH RAISE HORSES, BUT AH'VE WORKED CATTLE SOME AND DONE SOME PROSPECTIN'..
CAFE
CAFE

..AND YOU MIGHT AS WELL KNOW AH SERVED TIME IN PRISON.. FOR TAKIN' PART IN A BANK ROBBERY WHEN AH WAS A KID..

..BUT IF YOU'RE ASKIN' WHETHER AH'D BE A FIT GUARDIAN FOR FANCY, AH DON'T RECKON YOU COULD EVER FIND A BETTER ONE.

AH DON'T HAVE MUCH TO OFFER BUT MAHSELF, JUDGE..BUT SHE'LL HAVE ALL OF THAT FOR AS LONG AS AH LIVE.

AND WHAT ABOUT YOU, FANCY.. WOULD YOU LIKE MR. FAIRWEATHER HERE TO BE YOUR LEGAL GUARDIAN?
MORE THAN ANYTHING, JUDGE..HE'S HONEST, BRAVE, STRONG..AND I THINK HE LOVES ME!

I SEE. THANK YOU FOR YOUR HONESTY. I SHALL CONSIDER ALL THE FACTS IN THIS CASE..

..AND RENDER MY DECISION TOMORROW IN COURT. MEANWHILE, HAVE A GOOD EVENING.
MUCH OBLIGED, JUDGE..
..AND THANKS FOR SUPPER!

OH, FOOTLOOSE, I'M SO GLAD YOU'RE ALL RIGHT, AND THAT MR. SLAGG DIDN'T HURT YOU!
AH'M GLAD YOU SLIPPED ME THAT RAZOR, PUNKIN..

..IT GOT ME OUT O' THEM ROPES AND HELPED ME SUPRISE OL' BODIE PRETTY GOOD.

AH THUMPED ON HIM SOME AND SENT HIM RUNNIN' THROUGH THE STREETS O' DENVER IN HIS UNDERWEAR.

LAST AH SEEN OF HIM, HE WAS IN THE HANDS OF THE LOCAL POLICE, TRYIN' TO EXPLAIN. AH'LL BET HE STILL IS.

AFTER THOROUGH INVESTIGATION OF ALL THE FACTS IN THIS CASE, IT IS THE DECISION OF THIS COURT..

..THAT MR. FOOTLOOSE FAIRWEATHER BE GRANTED FULL LEGAL CUSTODY OF THE MINOR CHILD, FANCY FREE...

..AND THAT, IN COMPLIANCE WITH HER REQUEST, MR. FAIRWEATHER BE NAMED EXECUTOR OF MISS FREE'S ESTATE.

WITH REGARD TO MR. AND MRS. BELL, MISS FREE DECLINES TO PRESS CHARGES ON THE CRIMINAL MATTERS PRESENTLY UNDER INVESTIGATION, AS DOES MR. FAIRWEATHER.

HOWEVER, IT IS HEREWITH ORDERED THAT MR. AND MRS. BELL PAY ALL COURT COSTS AND LEGAL FEES INCURRED IN THIS CASE..
..AND THAT THEY REFRAIN FROM FURTHER CONTACT OF ANY FORM..WITH MISS FREE.
COURT IS ADJOURNED!

THIS CHEST SEEMS TO CONTAIN MOSTLY PERSONAL ITEMS, FANCY.. CLOTHING, A POCKET WATCH, DAGUERREOTYPES OF YOUR MOTHER AND YOU..
SF

..AND A DRAFT ON THE MINERS' BANK FOR $50,000, WHICH I UNDERSTAND YOU WISH PLACED IN A TRUST FUND.
THAT'S RIGHT, JUDGE.. WE FIGURE IT'LL HELP WITH FANCY'S EDUCATION.
MINERS BANK
DENVER, COLORADO
Fancy Tree
FIFTY THOUSAND
$50,000.00
Maynard Sutter, Pres.

A WISE CHOICE..BUT IT SHOULD DO MUCH MORE THAN THAT. IT HAS BEEN A PLEASURE TO MEET YOU BOTH, AND I WISH YOU EVERY HAPPINESS.
LIKEWISE, JUDGE.. IF YOU'RE EVER UP MONTANA WAY, LOOK US UP!

WELL, PUNKIN'..EVER'THIN' SEEMS TO BE SETTLED HERE..WHAT D' YOU SAY WE GET ON BACK TO OUR CABIN IN THE MOUNTAINS?
THAT SOUNDS WONDERFUL FOOTLOOSE..

..BIG CITIES ARE ALL RIGHT, FAR AS THEY GO..THEY JUST GO TOO FAR.
37

WELL, COWBOY..LOOKS LIKE YOU GOT LUCKY AN' WON ALL THE CHIPS IN THIS GAME.. BUT I'M CURIOUS..
..I'D LIKE TO KNOW YOUR REAL INTEREST IN OUR GIRL..BESIDES HER MONEY..AND WHY YOU DIDN'T PREFER CHARGES AGAINST ME FOR ASSAULT. WHAT ARE YOU TRYIN' TO PROVE?
WHY, NOTHIN' JINGLE..AH JUST DON'T BELIEVE IN PUTTIN' THE LAW ON A MAN..
AH DRUTHER HANDLE THINGS PERSONAL!
WHAP!
GOOD GOSH, FOOTLOOSE..DO YOU THINK HE'S SERIOUSLY HURT?
NAW..HE'S JUST RESTIN' FROM ATTACKIN' MAH HAND WITH HIS JAW..
..BUT AH'M FEELIN' GENEROUS TODAY.. AH'M STILL NOT GONNA PREFER CHARGES.
38.

HOOLIGAN MER
SAL
BEER
INTERMOUNTAIN STAGE LINE

WELL..HOOLIGAN HASN'T CHANGED ALL THAT MUCH.
EVEN THIS TOWN'S TOO BIG FOR ME, GIRL..

OOMS
..THE BEST THING ABOUT TRAVELING IS THE COMIN' BACK PART.

..LET'S GET OUR HORSES FROM THE LIVERY STABLE AND GET ON BACK TO THE HIGH COUNTRY.
SOUNDS GOOD TO ME, FOOTLOOSE..

IT SURE IS GOOD TO BE
HOME, FOOTLOOSE..
YOU'RE SURE YOU DON'T
FEEL DIFFERENT ABOUT
ME NOW THAT I'M AN
HEIRESS?
NAW, FANCY
AH LIKE YOU
ANYWAY.

Other products by Stan Lynde

Write for a free catalog of Stan Lynde products (prints, cards, T-shirts, old west clothing, etc.) and receive the quarterly newsletter "The COTTONWOOD CLARION" a newsletter for Stan Lynde friends and fans.

COTTONWOOD GRAPHICS, INC.
c/o Stan Lynde's OLD WEST MERCANTILE
410 E. 2nd St.
P.O. Box 848
Whitefish, MT 59937-0848
(1-800-937-6343)